Better Homes and Gardens®

The Best-Ever Gift

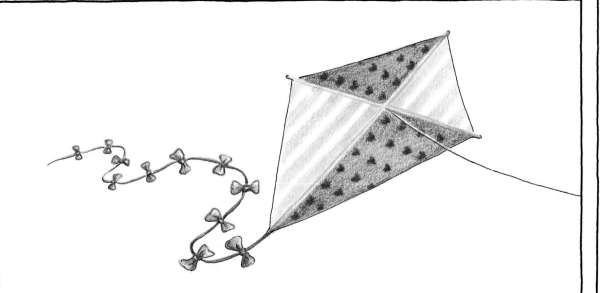

"Hi! Where's Max?" Elliot asked Marci, who was playing with Ozzy and Sara Jo.

"He's sick," Marci said.

"Sick! But he promised to help me fly my new kite!"

Yesterday, Max, Marci's older brother, had helped Elliot make a great kite. And today they were going to fly it—just the two of them.

"Oh, let's see your kite," Sara Jo said.

Elliot smiled proudly as he showed it to her. "Max helped me, but I made most of it myself."

"Neat! Let's try it!" said Sara Jo, and she took off with the kite.

"That's *MY* kite!" sputtered Elliot.

"I'll bring it back," she said, giggling as the kite sailed out behind her.

Elliot sighed and turned to go home. "At least it flies," he said.

"Want to play?" Ozzy called after him.

"Not now. Maybe later." And Elliot slowly walked away.

"I wish I could do something to make Max feel better," Elliot thought as he sat on his porch steps. "What could I make?"

Then he had an idea.

"Peanut butter cookies!" Elliot shouted.

Peanut butter was Elliot's favorite food. He put it on bread. He spread it on bananas. And once he even mixed it with his peas! He said it made them taste good, and he liked how it stopped the peas from rolling off his fork. Elliot and his mom made cookies out of peanut butter, too.

"Max will love these!" Elliot thought as he mixed the cookies. "And when I finish, I'm going to make Max a card—a silly card that will make him laugh."

When the cookies were done, Elliot got out
his crayons, paper, and glue. He got out his
scissors, paints, and some yarn. And he
colored, and he painted, and he pasted, and
he cut. As he worked, he thought up a funny
poem. His mom helped him spell the words.

Go fly a kite that's what I say.
Go fly a kite but not today.
Today you're sick. Your head is dizzy.
Your tongue is green. Your toes are frizzy
I hope you feel better soon!

Then Elliot printed his name in big letters.

Elliot was so excited. He could hardly wait
for Max to see the cookies and card! "Won't
Max be surprised," Elliot thought as he
skipped along.

But halfway to Max's house, Elliot saw
Vera huffing and puffing down the street
pulling her wagon. In it sat a large pot.
Vera's long ears flopped from side to side as
she tried to hurry.

"Elliot!" Vera called. "You've simply got to
help me. It's an emergency!"

"What's wrong?" asked Elliot.

"It's Mother's spring garden party. She
made this perfectly *marvelous* chicken
soup—gallons of it. But she forgot to make
dessert! And the guests arrive in *fifteen
minutes*!"

"Then why do you have her soup in your wagon?" Elliot asked.

"Mother thought I could trade the extra soup for some special cookies at the bakery."

"I made cookies for Max," Elliot said. And he proudly held up his box of cookies.

"Let me see," said Vera. She peered into the box. "Why, they're just perfect! Here. We'll trade." And off she ran with the cookies, leaving Elliot with the wagon and the pot of chicken soup.

"Come back! Those cookies are for Max," Elliot shouted.

But Vera was already gone.

"Oh, great!" said Elliot, pulling Vera's wagon toward Max's house. He was trying *so* hard not to spill the soup that he didn't see Bruno until he bumped into him.

"Hey, Elliot! Watch where you're going!"

Elliot looked up in surprise. "I'm sorry, Bruno. But I've got to get to Max's. He's sick and has to stay home."

"What's that in the wagon?" Bruno asked.

"Soup," said Elliot. And he told Bruno how Vera had traded it to him for the cookies.

"At least I still have my card," said Elliot.

"Card? Oh, no! My mom told me to get a card for Dad's birthday. And I forgot," groaned Bruno.

"I made this one for Max," Elliot said.

"Hey, this is great! Dad will love it!"

"It's for Max!"

"But I need it. PL-E-E-E-ASE!" insisted Bruno. "Besides, you traded with Vera. It's not fair if you don't trade with me.

"Here," he said, shoving a box of tissues at Elliot. "Now we're even!" And he left with the card, lumbering down the street as fast as his short legs could carry him.

Elliot felt like crying as he rang Max's doorbell. *Ding, dong.* He didn't have anything for Max. From inside he heard a big sneeze. "AH-CHOO!"

Max opened the door and sneezed again. He looked miserable.

AH·CHOO!

"I'm so sorry you're sick," Elliot said.

"I feel terrible," said Max. "All I do is blow my nose. And I just used my last tissue!"

"Oh!" said Elliot, surprised. "I have tissues." He handed Max the box Bruno had given him.

Max quickly grabbed a tissue just in time for an even bigger "AHHH-CHOO!"

"Bless you!" said Elliot.

"Thanks," said Max. "Now all I need is some chicken soup. That's what my grandma said I should eat to make me feel better."

Elliot's mouth dropped open. "Well, I have that, too!" he said. "Right here!" And he pointed to the large pot in Vera's wagon.

Max looked as surprised as Elliot. It was
THE BEST-EVER GIFT! "You're quite a
friend, Elliot!"

The small dragon smiled.

"I'll tell you what," Max said. "I'm sorry I
can't help you fly your kite today. But as
soon as I'm better, we'll fly it—just the two
of us."

Elliot grinned. *"All right!"* he said.

And that's exactly what they did.

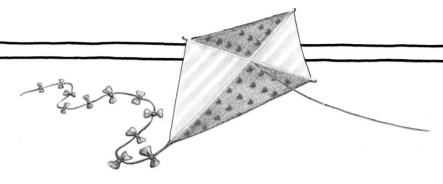

Fun-to-Fly Kites

There's no trick to flying this tissue-paper kite. Just look at Elliot!

What you'll need...

- Pencil
- One 8x12-inch piece of tissue paper or lightweight paper, folded in half
- Scissors
- 2 drinking straws
- Tape
- Paper punch
- 2 pieces of yarn or string, each about 25 inches long

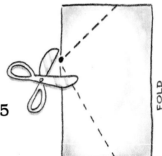

1 With adult help, use a pencil to draw the shape of the kite on your paper (see illustration, above). Use the scissors to cut out the kite.

Lay the straws on the kite between the top and bottom corners on both sides of the kite. Tape both ends of each straw to the kite (see photo).

2 Place a piece of tape on both sides of the 2 points of the kite. With adult help, use a paper punch to punch a hole *through the tape* on each point (see photo). Tie 1 piece of yarn to each hole. Tie the 2 pieces of yarn together about halfway between the kite and the end of the yarn.

Peanutty Chocolate Drops

You don't need to bake these cookies. They "cook" in the refrigerator.

What you'll need...

- 1 small saucepan
- 12 ounces chocolate-flavored confectioners' coating, cut up

- Measuring cups
- ¾ cup peanut butter
- Large mixing bowl
- 2 cups honey graham cereal

- 1 cup tiny marshmallows
- 1 cookie sheet
- Waxed paper
- 2 small spoons

1 In a small saucepan, put the confectioners' coating and peanut butter (see photo). With adult help, heat over medium heat till confectioners' coating and peanut butter have melted. Use a wooden spoon to stir the mixture occasionally.

2 In a large mixing bowl, put the cereal and marshmallows. With adult help, pour the melted peanut butter mixture over the cereal. Stir with a spoon till the cereal and marshmallows are covered with the peanut butter mixture (see photo). Cover a cookie sheet with waxed paper.

3 With a small spoon, scoop up some of the cookie mixture. Use another small spoon to push the cookie onto the cookie sheet (see photo). Chill the cookies about 20 minutes or till firm. Cover and store in the refrigerator. Makes about 36 cookies.

Fruity Cards

Gelatin adds bright colors and a fruity smell to your special greeting cards.

What you'll need...

- Construction paper, folded in half
- Markers, crayons, or colored pencils
- White crafts glue
- Fruit-flavored gelatin

1 Open the paper up and lay it flat. With markers, decorate the inside of the card any way you like. Fold the paper in half. On the front of the card, use glue to draw a design (see photo).

2 Sprinkle the gelatin over the glue (see photo). Make sure it completely covers all the glue. Let the glue dry for a few minutes. Shake off the excess gelatin. Let card dry completely.

Fun-to-Fly Kites

You can create a brightly colored kite by using paper or plastic that already has a design printed on it. Look for gift wrap, shopping bags, or plastic bags.

When you've played hard at flying your kite all day, fly one of these yummy bars right into your tummy.

Chewy Granola Kite Bars

    1   10-ounce bag marsh-
        mallows
    ¼   cup margarine or
        butter
    4   cups granola with
        raisins
    1½ cups crisp rice cereal
    ½   cup sunflower nuts

● Line a 13x9x2-inch pan with foil. Butter the foil. Set aside.
● In a large saucepan combine the marshmallows and margarine or butter. Cook and stir the mixture till the marshmallows are melted.
● Stir in granola, crisp rice cereal, and sunflower nuts.
● Press mixture into pan.

Cool. Remove foil lining with uncut bars from pan. Cut into diamond-shaped bars (see below). Makes 24.

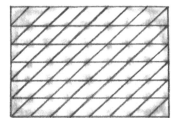

Peanutty Chocolate Drops

Don't despair if your cupboard is bare. Look for these foods to use instead of the ones listed on page 29.

Instead of the chocolate-flavored confectioners' coating, use one 12-ounce package semisweet or milk chocolate pieces. (If you use the chocolate pieces, be sure to eat the cookies right after you take them out of the refrigerator. The chocolate softens quickly.)

Also, lots of cereals work in these tasty cookies. Try round toasted oat cereal, crispy corn and rice cereal, or puffed corn cereal.

Fruity Cards

If red is your favorite color, use cherry-flavored gelatin. Our kid-testers found it gives the brightest red color. Also, if you have powdered drink mix at home, it will work in place of the gelatin. Just stir some sugar or salt into the drink mix to make it go further.

Decorate old greeting cards with gelatin, too. Put glue on the card where you want the gelatin to stick.

BETTER HOMES AND GARDENS® BOOKS
Editor: Gerald M. Knox   Art Director: Ernest Shelton   Managing Editor: David A. Kirchner
Department Head, Family Life: Sharyl Heiken

THE BEST-EVER GIFT
Editors: Jennifer Darling and Sandra Granseth   Graphic Designers: Brenda Lesch and Linda Vermie
Editorial Project Manager: Angela K. Renkoski
Contributing Writer: Nancy Buss   Contributing Illustrator: Buck Jones
Contributing Color Artist: Sue Fitzpatrick Cornelison   Contributing Photographer: Scott Little

Have BETTER HOMES AND GARDENS® magazine delivered to your door.
For information, write to: ROBERT AUSTIN, P.O. BOX 4536, DES MOINES, IA 50336